This book belongs to:

_____

_____

_____

First published 2015 by Walker Books Ltd
87 Vauxhall Walk, London SE11 5HJ

2 4 6 8 10 9 7 5 3

© 1990 – 2015 Lucy Cousins
Lucy Cousins font © 1990 – 2015 Lucy Cousins

The author/illustrator has asserted her moral rights

Illustrated in the style of Lucy Cousins by King Rollo Films Ltd

Maisy™. Maisy is a trademark of Walker Books Ltd, London

Printed in China

British Library Cataloguing in Publication Data:
a catalogue record for this book is
available from the British Library.

ISBN 978-1-4063-5872-8

www.walker.co.uk

Maisy Goes by Plane

Lucy Cousins

WALKER BOOKS
AND SUBSIDIARIES
LONDON • BOSTON • SYDNEY • AUCKLAND

When Maisy went to stay with Ella,
she went by plane. Ella lived so far away!
Cyril drove Maisy to the airport.
Maisy was very excited!

Maisy was in plenty of time to catch her flight.

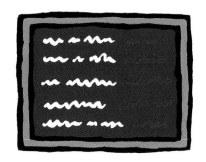

She showed her ticket and checked in her case.

Then she said goodbye to Cyril ...

"Goodbye!"

and went through security to the departure lounge.

All of the passengers began to board the plane. It was so exciting!

Maisy looked through to where the captain sat. Wow, it took a lot of lights and buttons to make a plane go!

Maisy eventually found her seat. "Row 1, 2, 3, ah here I am – row 10!" She had a window seat!

Maisy quickly made new friends with Mr Percy, who sat by the aisle, and Betsy, who sat in the middle!

Mr Percy pulled and **PULLED** to get his seat belt on and all three friends helped each other with their belts. **CLICK! CLICK! CLICK!**

The stewardess then talked about safety. Betsy seemed a little nervous so Maisy held her hand as the plane **WHOOSHED** down the runway!

Maisy felt the
plane lift off.

A steward
brought Maisy
a drink of
orange juice.

Betsy read
a magazine ...

ZZZZZZZZZzzzz

and Mr Percy
went to sleep.

But Maisy
needed to go
to the toilet...

Some of the passengers walked up and down the aisle, while Maisy queued up

to use the toilet. She had to squeeze
really hard to get inside. It was so tiny!

The plane soared on and on through the night sky, until a loud voice came through the speaker: "Soon we will be landing!"

Everyone had to return to their seats, put their seat backs up and their seat belts on.

Touchdown! The plane gave a little bump and a jump as it landed.

"Hooray!" Many passengers cheered and clapped and Maisy joined in.

They had flown so far
in just a few hours!

Maisy thanked the crew and the captain as she got off the plane.

Maisy, Betsy and Mr Percy waited

together to collect their bags.

Then there was Ella! "Hello, Ella!
Goodbye, Mr Percy and Betsy."
What a fun flight it had been!